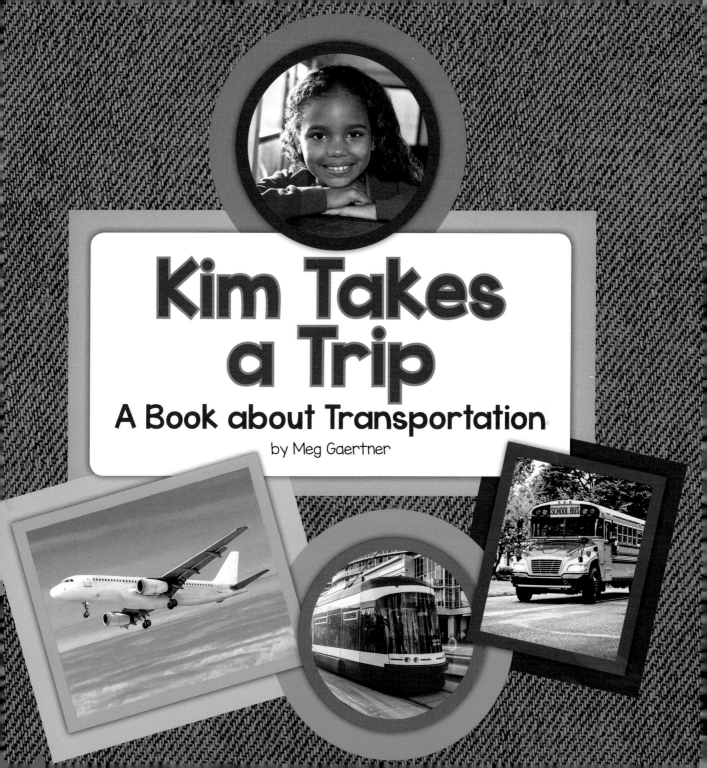

Kim Takes a Trip
A Book about Transportation
by Meg Gaertner

The Child's World®
childsworld.com

Published by The Child's World®
1980 Lookout Drive • Mankato, MN 56003-1705
800-599-READ • www.childsworld.com

Photographs ©: iStockphoto, cover (top), cover (bottom middle),
cover (bottom left), 1 (top), 1 (bottom left), 1 (bottom middle),
3, 4, 7, 18, 21; Stuart Monk/Shutterstock Images, cover
(bottom right), 1 (bottom right); Ken Hurst/Shutterstock Images,
8; William Perugini/Shutterstock Images, 11; Taras Vyshnya/
Shutterstock Images, 12; Shutterstock Images, 15, 16

ISBN HARDCOVER: 9781503827509
ISBN PAPERBACK: 9781622434299
LCCN: 2017964163

Printed in the United States of America • PA02388

About the Author

Meg Gaertner is a children's book author and
editor who lives in Minnesota. When not writing,
she enjoys dancing and spending time outdoors.

Today was a big day for Kim.
What happened to Kim today?

Kim went on a fun trip after school.
First she got on a school bus.

She rode the bus with her friends.
The bus took them home.

Then Kim walked to a **train** station with her mom. They got on a train.

The train took them to the **airport**.

At the airport, Kim got on an **airplane**. The airplane flew off the ground.

Kim had fun looking out the window. She saw clouds. The world looked so small from high above!

The airplane landed in a different city.

Kim's dad was there to meet her!

Have you ever taken a big trip?

Glossary

airplane (AIR-plane) An airplane is a large machine with wings that can fly through the air. People ride in an airplane to get from one place to another.

airport (AIR-port) An airport is a place where people get on and off airplanes. Airplanes lift off the ground at an airport and fly to a different city.

train (TRANE) A train is a line of railroad cars that move together on a track. People can ride in a train, or a train can carry things from one place to another.

Extended Learning Activities

1. When was the last time you went on a trip? Where did you go on the trip? How did you get there?

2. Kim went on a school bus, a train, and an airplane. What forms of transportation do you take each day?

3. Kim traveled to see her dad. Do any of your family members live far away? Where do they live?

To Learn More

Books

Biggs, Brian. *On Land*. New York, NY: Balzer + Bray, 2011.

Gibbons, Gail. *Transportation: How People Get Around*. New York, NY: Holiday House, 2017.

Oxlade, Chris. *A Journey through Transport*. London, England: QEB Publishing, 2017.

Web Sites

Visit our Web site for links about transportation:

childsworld.com/links

Note to Parents, Teachers, and Librarians: We routinely verify our Web links to make sure they are safe, active sites—so encourage your readers to check them out!